The Boy Who Cried Wolf

Retold By
Freya Littledale

Pictures By
James Marshall

SCHOLASTIC INC.
New York Toronto London Auckland Sydney

For Glenn and Harold
—FREYA LITTLEDALE

For Harry Allard
—JAMES MARSHALL

Based on a fable from Aesop

0-590-40310-9

12 11 10 9 8 7 6 5   1/9   08

Once there was a shepherd boy called Tom.

Day after day

he sat on a hill

and watched his sheep.

Night after night he went home,
ate his supper, and fell asleep.

"Nothing ever happens to me," thought Tom.
"I see hunters hunt in the woods
and fishermen fish in the lake.
But I just sit here and watch my sheep."

And so he did.

He watched the sheep eat the grass.

He watched them sleep in the sun.

He watched them follow the leader
along the side of the hill.

One morning Tom was watching his sheep
when he saw some hunters
walking through the woods.
"Today I'll have some fun," said he.
And he began to yell,
"Help! Help! Help!
A wolf is going to eat my sheep."

"Don't be afraid," shouted the hunters.
"We're coming."
And they ran out of the woods
with their great big guns.

"Where's the wolf?" they asked.

"Follow me," said Tom.
And he led the hunters down to the lake . . .
and all around it.

"We don't see the wolf," they said.

"He must have gone back to my sheep,"
said Tom.

And he led the hunters back to the sheep.

"Baaaaaaa," went the sheep.

"There is no wolf!" shouted the hunters.

"Haaaaaaaa!" laughed Tom.
"You're right.
There is no wolf.
I fooled you!"

The hunters were very angry.
"You'll never fool us again!" they said.
And off they went
back into the woods.

The next morning Tom was watching his sheep,
when he saw some fishermen down by the lake.
"I'll have more fun today!" thought Tom.
And he began to yell,
"Help! Help! Help!
A wolf is going to eat my sheep."

"Don't worry," shouted the fishermen,
"we'll help you."
And they ran all the way up the hill.

"Where's the wolf?" they asked.

"I saw him go into the woods," said Tom.
"Follow me."
And he led the fishermen into the woods . . .
and out again.

"There is no wolf," said the fishermen.

"Ha! Ha! Ha!" Tom laughed.
"You're right.
There is no wolf.
I fooled you!"

The fishermen were very angry.
"We have better things to do
than look for a wolf that isn't there."
And they went back to the lake
to catch some fish.

"Oh, that was fun!" laughed Tom.
"I wish I could do it every day."

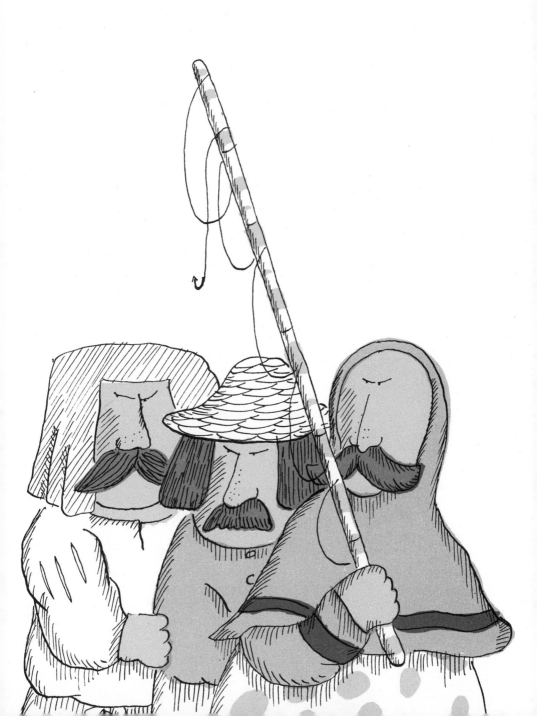

The very next morning
Tom was watching his sheep
when he heard a horrible howl.

"Who's there?" Tom called.
"Is it one of you men
playing a trick on *me*?"
But no one answered.

Then all at once Tom saw a
great big wolf standing by his side.

"I like your sheep," said the wolf.
"I think I'll eat them for lunch."

"You can't do that!" said Tom.

"Yes I can," said the wolf.

"No you can't!" cried Tom.
"I'm going to get help!"

And he ran all the way down to town.

"WOLF! WOLF! WOLF!" Tom cried.

The people of the town came running.
The hunters and the fishermen came too

"A wolf is going to eat my sheep!"
called Tom. "Come with me!"

"No!" said the hunters.
"You fooled us before!"

"You fooled us too!" said the fishermen.

"We heard all about you,"
said the people of the town.
"And you can't fool anyone here!"

"But I'm not fooling this time," Tom cried.
"I'm telling the truth.
Follow me and you'll see."

"We don't believe you!" shouted the hunters.

"You tricked us!" shouted the fishermen.

"Go back to your sheep!"
shouted everyone else in town.

"Oh my!" said Tom,
"what can I do now?"
And he left the town
and ran back up the hill.

He looked and looked and looked.
But he could not find a single sheep.
The wolf had eaten them all.

"Nobody came to help me," cried Tom.
"And now my sheep are gone."

Then all at once
he heard the wolf.

"Heh! Heh! Heh!" laughed the wolf.
"You told so many lies
no one believed you
when you told the truth!"

And away he went
deep into the woods.

"The wolf is right," thought Tom.
"I must tell the truth."
And from that time on,
he always did.